DREAMWORKS

HOW TO TRAIN YOUR DRAGON

THE HIDDEN WORLD

THE MOVIE STORYBOOK

Adapted by May Nakamura
Illustrated by Michelle Lam

Simon Spotlight
New York   London   Toronto   Sydney   New Delhi

SIMON SPOTLIGHT

An imprint of Simon & Schuster Children's Publishing Division

1230 Avenue of the Americas, New York, New York 10020

This Simon Spotlight edition January 2019

How to Train Your Dragon: The Hidden World © 2019 DreamWorks Animation LLC. All Rights Reserved.

All rights reserved, including the right of reproduction in whole or in part in any form.

SIMON SPOTLIGHT and colophon are registered trademarks of Simon & Schuster, Inc.

For information about special discounts for bulk purchases, please contact Simon & Schuster Special Sales at
1-866-506-1949 or business@simonandschuster.com.

Manufactured in China 1118 LEO

10 9 8 7 6 5 4 3 2 1 • ISBN 978-1-5344-3813-2 • ISBN 978-1-5344-3814-9 (eBook)

"This . . . is Berk," Hiccup said happily. The village was looking just as he'd always hoped it would—full of dragons roaming freely. There were so many dragons—Stormcutters, Gronckles, Thunderdrums, and more—that they outnumbered the Vikings!

Hiccup smiled. He was proud to be the chief of a village where humans and dragons lived together in peace.

Suddenly, Toothless, Hiccup's Night Fury dragon, heard a strange groaning in the distance. He followed the sound and found a small clearing in the forest. There, a beautiful Light Fury dragon was crouched by a trap. She looked just like Toothless except her scales were white.

The Light Fury warned Toothless about the trap with a low growl. Then they started purring at each other.

When Hiccup and his friend Astrid appeared, the Light Fury was startled. "We're friends!" called Hiccup, but the Light Fury took off into the sky and disappeared.

Toothless was in love, but he didn't know when he would ever see the Light Fury again. Hiccup searched around the clearing to look for clues. He found a vial filled with a mysterious green liquid.

Back at the village, Hiccup showed his friends what he had found.

Eret looked at the vial. "I know this handiwork," he said. "Grimmel. The smartest dragon hunter I've ever met."

"Can't be that smart," said Hiccup. "He left his trap unmanned."

"Don't underestimate him, Hiccup," warned Eret. "Mark my words. He'll be back."

Hiccup loved Berk, but it was no longer a safe place to live. Grimmel could arrive and attack at any moment.

"We are exposed and vulnerable," Hiccup said. "If we want to live in peace with our dragons, we have to disappear off the map—take the dragons to a place where no one will find them."

Hiccup remembered a tale that his father, Stoick, had told him when he was young. "Out there, beyond the sunset," Stoick would say, "lies the home of the dragons. . . . Sailors who turned back told tales of a great waterfall and dragons guarding the entrance to a Hidden World. Not just a nest, Hiccup, but a land from which all dragons come."

Hiccup wanted to find the Hidden World and turn it into a new home for the people and dragons of Berk! "Berk is more than this place," he told the Vikings. "We are Berk. The people, the dragons. I say Berk is wherever we go."

So all the Vikings packed their belongings and left Berk with the dragons. The only plan was to keep flying until they reached the end of the world!

Suddenly, Astrid pointed toward the clouds. "The Light Fury!" she said.

"Looks like she's following us!" said Hiccup's mother, Valka. Toothless chased after the Light Fury, but the dragon magically vanished into thin air.

"Where'd she go? Is she made of sky?" Tuffnut asked.

Soon the dragons—and the Vikings—became tired. The Berkians stopped to rest on a towering island in the middle of the sea and fell in love with it right away. It had everything: forests, waterfalls, and a beautiful valley.

"Say hello to New Berk!" announced a Viking named Hoark.

Hiccup agreed to build a temporary village on the island and stay until they could find the Hidden World, but he knew that they still weren't safe from Grimmel.

At his new workbench, Hiccup made an automatic tail fin for Toothless.

"You tried this once before. He didn't want it," Astrid said.

"Until now, he didn't have a reason to," Hiccup said. "He's my best bud. I want him to be happy." If the Light Fury appeared again, Hiccup wanted Toothless to be able to fly on his own.

At night, the Light Fury visited New Berk, and she and Toothless flew side by side! She showed Toothless how she used secret cloaking powers to seemingly disappear: First she blasted a fireball, and then she flew through it and vanished. Toothless tried cloaking himself too, but it didn't work. He was frustrated.

Toothless and the Light Fury flew long and far together. Finally, they reached a circle of waterfalls on the edge of a crater that met the surface of the sea, forming a giant hole in the ocean. The Light Fury dove into the hole, and Toothless followed.

Back at New Berk, Hiccup worried that Grimmel would attack while Toothless was gone with the Light Fury. Hiccup decided to try to capture Grimmel, but when he and his friends went to Grimmel's fort, Raven Point, they stumbled right into a trap!

"You're nothing without your dragon," Grimmel sneered at Hiccup.

Luckily, almost everyone escaped, except Ruffnut. The mission was a complete failure.

Hiccup was discouraged. He wondered if Grimmel was right—maybe he wasn't capable of protecting the village on his own. He needed to find Toothless and bring him back right away.

"I never thought he'd stay away for good," Hiccup said. "I shouldn't have let him go."

So Hiccup, Astrid, and her dragon, Stormfly, set out. Stormfly was a tracker dragon, and she was their best hope for finding Toothless.

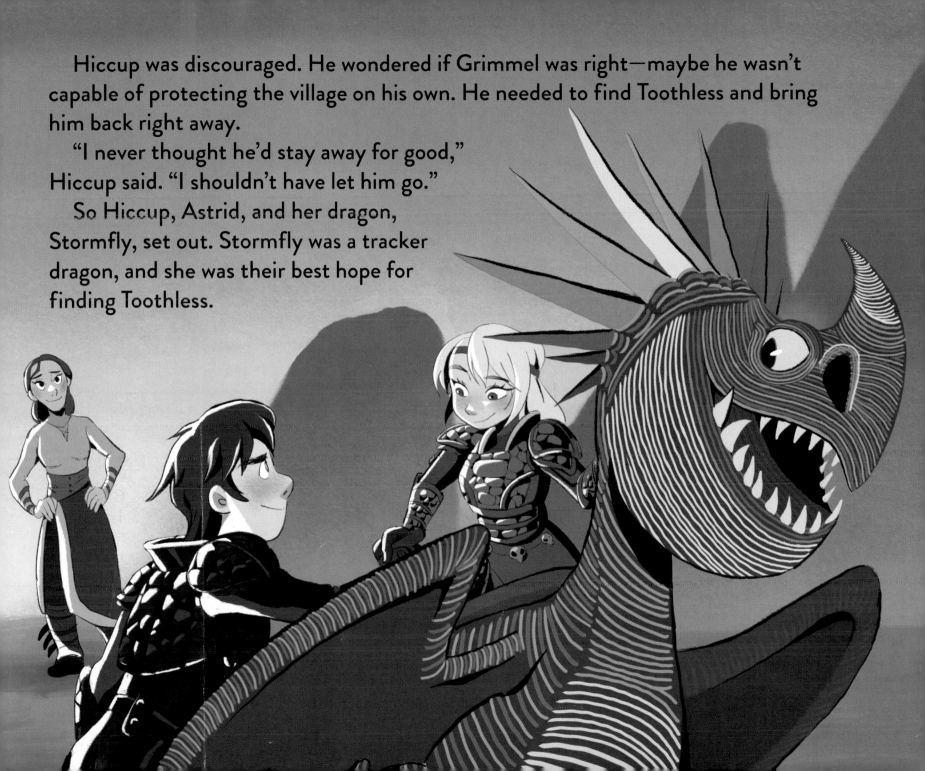

After a while, Stormfly found the hole in the middle of the sea. They dove in and discovered . . . the legendary Hidden World of dragons!

"It really does exist!" Hiccup said.

It was a breathtaking sight. Thousands of different dragons roamed and flew across the cavernous, mysterious land. There were coral and crystal structures everywhere.

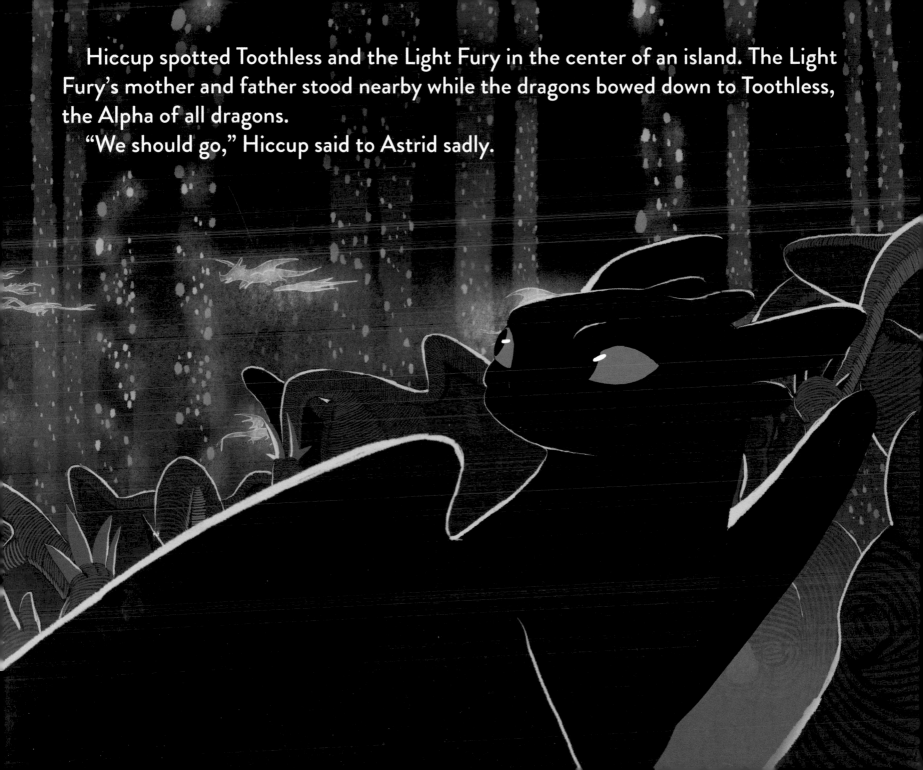

Hiccup spotted Toothless and the Light Fury in the center of an island. The Light Fury's mother and father stood nearby while the dragons bowed down to Toothless, the Alpha of all dragons.

"We should go," Hiccup said to Astrid sadly.

Toothless noticed Hiccup, Astrid, and Stormfly, and he rescued them from dragons in the Hidden World who were fearful of humans. He flew them back to New Berk. Later, Hiccup realized that the Light Fury had followed Toothless.

"It's okay," Hiccup said to Toothless. "You belong in the Hidden World. We don't."

Toothless looked around New Berk. Then he looked at the Light Fury. He didn't know where to go.

Suddenly, Ruffnut arrived. She had escaped from Grimmel. "Miss me?" she asked.

Unfortunately, Ruffnut had also led Grimmel straight to New Berk! Grimmel captured all the dragons there and tried to escape. Hiccup and his friends chased after him, burning ships and fighting against Grimmel's menacing Deathgripper dragons. One by one, the Vikings were able to free their dragons, and Grimmel realized that he could not win the battle. He used the mysterious green liquid from one of the vials on the Light Fury, and it made her follow all his orders.

"Go!" he yelled, jumping onto her back.

Hiccup and Toothless flew after Grimmel. But they couldn't attack without hurting the Light Fury too. Meanwhile, the Deathgrippers were catching up behind them. Toothless concentrated. His dorsal plates split, and his scales—along with those on Hiccup's flight suit—became reflective like a mirror. Toothless commanded lightning from the storm clouds nearby to strike them since his scales were fireproof, and something amazing happened: Hiccup and Toothless vanished!

Hiccup was impressed with Toothless's new power. But then Grimmel, who was fast approaching on the Light Fury, fired a dart with the green liquid at them. Hiccup twisted in the air to avoid it and crashed into Grimmel. The dragon hunter was knocked off the Light Fury, but he still clung to Hiccup. The dart, which had pierced through Hiccup's Dragon Armor, hit Toothless directly. Toothless began to fall. Hiccup tore off the Light Fury's bridle with the vials of green liquid that kept her obedient to Grimmel.

"Save him," Hiccup said to her as he bravely let go. The Light Fury zoomed to rescue Toothless as Hiccup and Grimmel plummeted toward the ocean.

At the very last moment, the Light Fury swooped down and carried Hiccup to safety! Hiccup, Toothless, and their friends returned to New Berk. Everyone cheered. Then Hiccup cleared his throat. "It's time," he told Toothless. "I won't hold you back anymore. You've looked after us long enough. Time to look after yourselves."

The villagers gasped. But when Astrid unbuckled Stormfly's saddle, they followed her lead.

"Go, bud," Hiccup said to Toothless. "Lead them to the Hidden World. You'll be safer there. Safer than you could ever be with us."

Toothless nuzzled Hiccup's hand and purred. Then he roared and took off into the sky. The other dragons followed and disappeared from view as they headed toward the Hidden World.

"Legend says that when the ground quakes or lava spews from the earth, it's the dragons . . . letting us know they're still here waiting for us to figure out how to get along," Hiccup said. "The world believes the dragons are gone, if they ever existed at all. But we Berkians know otherwise."

Hiccup told the Vikings that they would guard the secret until the time comes . . . when dragons could finally return in peace.